STEP INTO READING® will help your child get there. The program offers five steps to reading success. Each step includes fun stories and colorful art or photographs. In addition to original fiction and books with favorite characters, there are Step into Reading Non-Fiction Readers, Phonics Readers and Boxed Sets, Sticker Readers, and Comic Readers—a complete literacy program with something to interest every child.

Learning to Read, Step by Step!

Ready to Read **Preschool–Kindergarten**
• big type and easy words • rhyme and rhythm • picture clues
For children who know the alphabet and are eager to begin reading.

Reading with Help **Preschool–Grade 1**
• basic vocabulary • short sentences • simple stories
For children who recognize familiar words and sound out new words with help.

Reading on Your Own **Grades 1–3**
• engaging characters • easy-to-follow plots • popular topics
For children who are ready to read on their own.

Reading Paragraphs **Grades 2–3**
• challenging vocabulary • short paragraphs • exciting stories
For newly independent readers who read simple sentences with confidence.

Ready for Chapters **Grades 2–4**
• chapters • longer paragraphs • full-color art
For children who want to take the plunge into chapter books but still like colorful pictures.

STEP INTO READING® is designed to give every child a successful reading experience. The grade levels are only guides; children will progress through the steps at their own speed, developing confidence in their reading. The F&P Text Level on the back cover serves as another tool to help you choose the right book for your child.

Remember, a lifetime love of reading starts with a single step!

For Laetitia, Isabelle, Cyrus, Emeline,
Frankie, Clara, Clark, and Elinor,
who all have teeth
—A.M.

To you, the reader—you're brilliant!
Happy reading!
—T.B.

Visit us on the Web!
StepIntoReading.com
rhcbooks.com

Educators and librarians, for a variety of teaching tools, visit us at RHTeachersLibrarians.com

Library of Congress Cataloging-in-Publication Data
Names: Membrino, Anna, author. | Budgen, Tim, illustrator.
Title: Big Shark, Little Shark, and the Missing Teeth / by Anna Membrino ;
illustrated by Tim Budgen.
Description: First edition. | New York : Random House Children's Books, [2022] |
Series: Step into reading. Step 1 | Audience: Ages 4–6. | Audience: Grades K–1. |
Summary: "While Big Shark loses another tooth, Little Shark is dolefully waiting to lose his first."
Identifiers: LCCN 2021033389 | ISBN 978-0-593-30210-1 (trade paperback) |
ISBN 978-0-593-30211-8 (library binding) | ISBN 978-0-593-30212-5 (ebook)
Subjects: CYAC: Sharks—Fiction. | Teeth—Fiction.
Classification: LCC PZ7.M5176 Bim 2022 | DDC [E]—dc23

Printed in the United States of America
10 9 8 7 6 5 4 3 2 1
First Edition

This book has been officially leveled by using the F&P Text Level Gradient™ Leveling System.

STEP INTO READING®

Big Shark, Little Shark, and the Missing Teeth

by Anna Membrino
illustrated by Tim Budgen

Random House New York

Big Shark.

Big teeth.

Little Shark.

Small teeth.

Big Shark has a

loose tooth.

Pop!

It fell out!

Sharks lose teeth
all the time.
Big Shark has lost
a lot of teeth.

Big Shark likes
to save his teeth.
He keeps them in
a big chest.

Little Shark has not lost any teeth yet.

Little Shark wants to lose a tooth like Big Shark.

One day,
Big Shark goes to
count the teeth.

Oh no.
The chest is empty.
The teeth are gone!

Big Shark looks all over for the missing teeth.

They are not
in the ship.

They are not
by the swing.

They are not
under the stingray.

Big Shark is sad.

Little Shark feels bad.

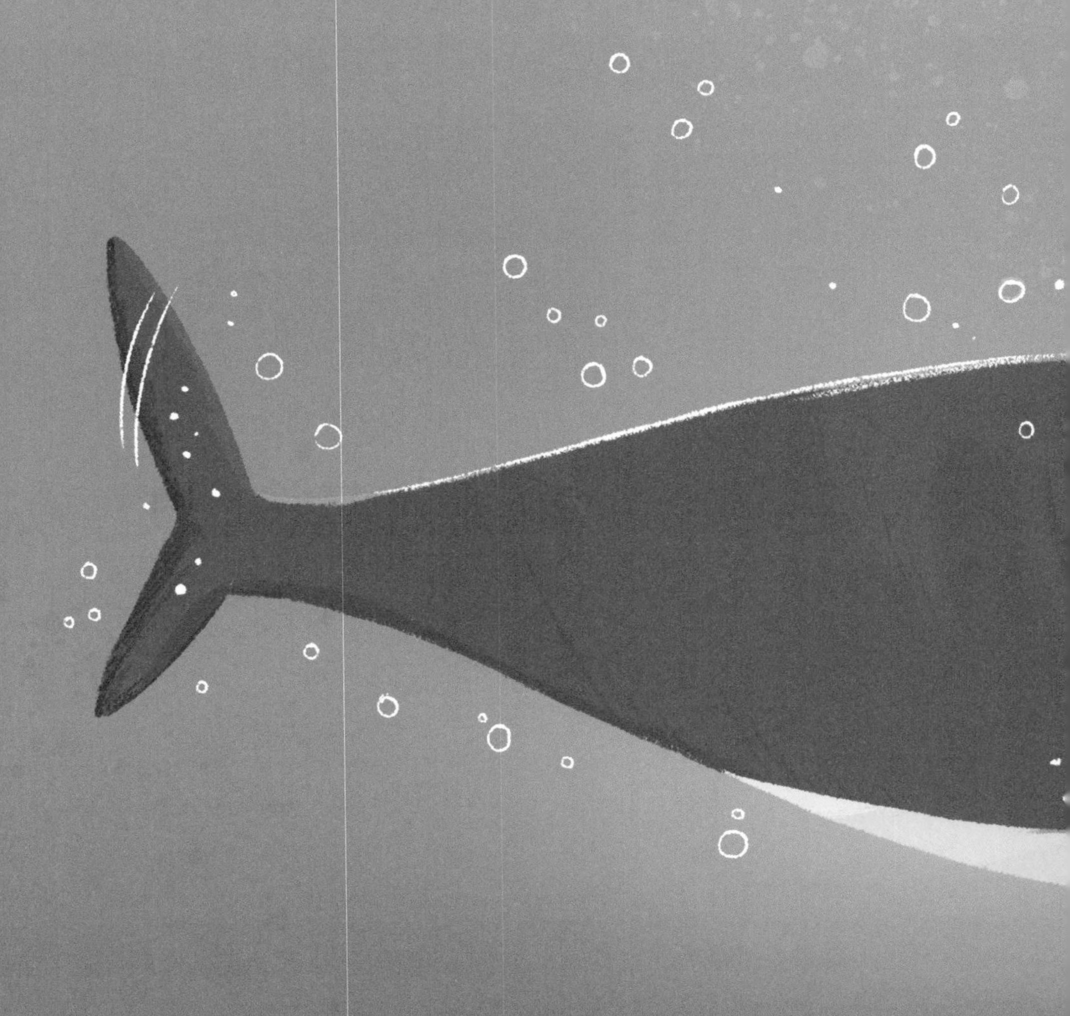

Little Shark knows
where the teeth are.

Little Shark shows Big Shark where he hid the teeth.

Little Shark is sorry for taking the teeth. Little Shark just wanted to be like Big Shark.

Big Shark has
an idea.

Big Shark gives
Little Shark an apple.
Take a bite,
Little Shark!

Hooray!
Little Shark lost
a tooth!